Reward for Muffin

Written by Jim Schembri

Illustrated by Gus Gordon

sundance

a black dog book

Published by
Sundance Publishing
P.O. Box 1326
234 Taylor Street
Littleton, MA 01460

First published 2001 by
Pearson Education Australia Pty. Limited
95 Coventry Street
South Melbourne 3205 Australia
Exclusive United States Distribution: Sundance Publishing

ISBN 0-7608-4997-8

Printed in China

Contents

Characters

Andy is a caring, friendly boy who loves cats a little too much.

Muffin is a lively kitten with lots of energy and a sticky nose.

Chapter One

Little Cat Lost

Andy was playing in the park.

A big piece of paper blew into his face.

He pulled it off and read it.

“That is so sad,” said Andy.
“I hope they find Muffin soon.”
He knew exactly how they felt.
Two weeks ago, Andy lost a kitten called Bing.
He searched and searched,
but he never saw him again.

Andy felt sorry for the family that lost Muffin.

Chapter Two

Little Cat Found

Andy saw something move in a tree.

It was a white kitten with a red collar.

The kitten looked scared.

“Muffin?” Andy said.

The kitten suddenly looked down at Andy.

Meow.

This must be Muffin, Andy thought.

“Here Muffin,” said Andy.

“Here kitty, kitty, kitty. Come to me, Muffin.”

Muffin meowed. Then Andy meowed.

Muffin meowed back.

Slowly, Muffin climbed down the tree

and walked up to Andy.

Muffin rubbed herself against Andy's legs.
Muffin began purring.
"Muffin really likes me," said Andy.
"Too bad I have to return her."

Andy picked up Muffin.
Andy felt Muffin's little claws digging into his sweater. He felt the kitten's heart beating. Then Muffin purred.

Andy looked into Muffin's eyes.
"I should take you home," said Andy.
"But it's getting late. We'll have to go to my house. You can spend the night, and we'll have lots of fun."

But nothing went as Andy planned.

Chapter Three
No Place Like Home

Muffin seemed to like Andy's house.

As soon as Andy walked in,

Muffin jumped out of his arms.

"Muffin! Come back!" Andy yelled.

But Muffin did not listen.
She ran into the kitchen.

Andy's mom was carrying a cake
to the kitchen table.
Mom tripped over the kitten.
The cake flew into the air.
It landed right on Andy's head!

Muffin ran into the living room.

Andy ran into the living room.

He still had cake all over his head!

Andy's brother, Carl, was watching TV.

He didn't see Muffin, but Muffin saw him.

The kitten jumped on Carl's head.

Carl screeched.

Muffin screeched back.

Andy's dad came in.

"What's all this noise?" he said.

Muffin jumped on Dad's back.

"Oww! It scratched me!" he shouted.

"Andy! Get that cat out of here!"

Andy tried to grab Muffin.

The kitten leaped onto the shelf.

"My glass animals!" Andy's dad yelled.

"They took years to collect!"

“Get that cat out!” Andy’s dad shouted again.

Andy chased Muffin into the backyard.

Muffin ran up a tree.

Andy put milk in a saucer.
He sat the saucer by the tree.
After a few minutes,
Muffin came down to drink it.
"Whew," said Andy.
But the trouble had just begun.

Chapter Four
The Howling

Andy thought Muffin would settle down for the night. He was wrong.

Muffin sat on the back fence and howled.

Muffin howled and howled.

Andy wondered how such a small kitten could make so much noise.

No one in the house could sleep.
No one on the whole street could sleep.
No one in the whole neighborhood
slept all night.

"Muffin must be homesick," Andy said.
"I better take her home."

Chapter Five
The Reward

Early the next morning, Andy took Muffin home. It was not easy because Muffin kept trying to get free.

Muffin clawed at Andy's sweater.

She tried to climb on Andy's head.

But Andy held Muffin tightly.

If she escaped, Muffin would be lost again.

Andy hurried to 45 Bell Street.

He knocked on the door, and a girl answered.

"Muffin!" the girl yelled with joy.

Muffin jumped into the girl's arms.

Andy could hear Muffin purr.

"Oh, thank you," the girl said to Andy.

“We must give you the reward,” the girl said.

Andy followed the girl into the house.
In the living room, Andy spotted a large basket
filled with a big cat and a litter of kittens.
They all looked exactly like Muffin.

“Please take a kitten as a reward,” said the girl.

“Are they all like Muffin?” Andy asked.

“Oh yes,” said the girl.

“No thanks,” said Andy, quickly. “Returning Muffin is reward enough.”

And Andy walked home,

happy that Muffin was back with her family.